Grandma introduced me to my friend *Jesus*

GRANDMA INTRODUCED ME TO MY FRIEND JESUS © 2020 by Kevin Lovegreen. All rights reserved. No part of this book may be reproduced in any form whatsoever, by photography or xerography or by any other means, by broadcast or transmission, by translation into any kind of language, nor by recording electronically or otherwise, without permission in writing from the author, except by a reviewer, who may quote brief passages in critical articles or reviews.

Softcover ISBN 13: 978-1-7346743-2-3

Printed in the United States of America
Second Printing: 2020

24 23 22 21 20   5 4 3 2 1

Cover and interior design by James Monroe Design, LLC.

Lucky Luke, LLC.
4335 Matthew Court
Eagan, Minnesota 55123

www.KevinLovegreen.com
Quantity discounts available!

A Note to the Reader

God chose me to write this book specially for you. It all began when I prayed for some way to get one hundred thousand books into kids' hands. At the time, I was thinking about Lucky Luke's Hunting Adventures, my award-winning book series.

Well, God heard my prayer and answered it. I will never forget that day. It was the first time I had a personal interaction with God.

Of all the places this could have happened, it ended up being in my bathroom. As I stood brushing my teeth, staring in the mirror, a vision started downloading into my mind. It was crystal clear as it played like a dream, but I was very awake. My brushing slowed as I focused in on the vision, trying to understand what was happening.

In the vision, my life passed by like a movie. Several things from my middle school years rolled through my mind. I realized these were memories I didn't want to recall. They were moments in time when I had made choices I'm not proud of today. They weren't terrible things—they were just typical, everyday school moments. But in each case, I could have chosen to treat my classmates better. For a moment, I thought God was scolding me for how I had acted.

Then the movie in my mind took an interesting turn. I was transported to my favorite place on earth: my grandparents' cabin in the woods. I could see the old red logs, I could smell the fire burning in the fireplace, and I could picture my grandmother's warm smile as she saw me coming through the front door.

As the vision ended, I just stood there with my toothbrush hanging from my mouth.

God then spoke to me as if He were inside my head: "You have been praying for one hundred thousand books, but it won't be with Lucky Luke's Hunting Adventures."

That's when I dropped my toothbrush in the sink and ran downstairs to tell my wife what had happened.

She simply smiled and said, "Sounds like you better get writing."

The more I thought about the vision and God's words, the more I believe He wanted me to show you how important His Son, Jesus, is to your life. This book is a story about one boy, one amazing grandmother, and one very important summer. I hope you enjoy it.

Chapter 1

Kevin was bursting with both relief and excitement as he raced off the bus and up his driveway. He was relieved seventh grade was over. Next year, he and his friends would be eighth graders—the kings of middle school.

A car pulled into the driveway, and Kevin's sister, Linda, hopped out. A friend's mom had given Linda and the friend a ride home from high school. There was no doubt—the look on Linda's face showed how relieved she was to put ninth grade behind her. Her class had been the youngest in the school. It would be way more fun next year.

But more importantly, Kevin and Linda were excited because the last day of school meant they'd be heading to their grandparents' cabin. For most of the year, Grandma and Bapoe lived twenty minutes away from Kevin and Linda. But now that they were retired, Grandma and Bapoe spent most of the summer at their cabin up north.

The whole family loved being at the cabin. Each year, summer vacation started with an extended week up there. Kevin could already picture the endless trees, the green grass, and that magical lake sitting at the bottom of the hill.

Little did Kevin know, this would be the most important summer of his life.

After a lightning-fast trip inside the house to drop off their backpacks, Kevin and Linda hopped into their dad's big silver SUV. It was loaded to the top with stuff for their cabin adventure. Mom and Dad would stay for the weekend, then head back home, giving Kevin and Linda the week alone with Grandma and Bapoe. Mom and Dad would return the following weekend to enjoy the cabin one more time before they all came home.

As usual, Dad was in the driver's seat. Mom planned to sing along with the radio or read her book most of the way up. Kevin and Linda were in the back seat. It would be a five-hour drive north, but looking forward to nine days of fun would hopefully make time pass quickly.

It didn't take long, however, for trouble to start. For some reason, Kevin kept touching Linda with his stinky socks. The madder she got, the funnier he thought it was.

"Stop it!" she snapped. Finally, she let out a plea for help: "Dad!"

Dad reached his boiling point. He spun around in his seat and pointed a finger right at Kevin. How he managed not to drive off the road was an amazing feat.

"Knock it off, Kevin!" he said, his voice raising. "If you don't, then I'm gonna pull this car over, and we're gonna have a serious talk."

Kevin got the message loud and clear. His heart sank once he realized how upset he had made his dad. But sometimes he just couldn't stop himself from picking on Linda—especially when he was bored.

Kevin wasn't your ordinary kid, although he was like a million other kids. Maybe even like you. Kevin's big smile and firecracker personality caused him to stand out in a crowd. Getting good grades was never a priority for him. But throwing touchdowns and crushing home runs—that, he loved. At five foot ten, he was an average-size kid, but he was fast and had a great arm. Being a jock made him very popular at school.

For the most part, Kevin was a good kid. But the way he treated others at school—and now in the back seat—had gotten him into trouble on more than one occasion. He was usually just looking for a laugh. Unfortunately, it was typically at the expense of someone else. Teachers, principals, and now Dad saw it as being disrespectful.

With a frown, Kevin grabbed his pillow and curled up against the door. Maybe it would be safer to just sleep the whole way to the cabin. He closed his eyes.

Seemingly moments later, the sound of rocks crunching beneath the tires woke him up. They were on a dirt road, and that could mean they were close to the cabin.

"Are we there?" Kevin asked, popping up.

"Almost," Mom said. "You managed to sleep most of the way, you lucky duck."

They turned off the dirt road and passed through a big green gate propped open with a log. They bounced down the long dirt driveway. Giant trees with bright-green leaves arched overhead, almost creating a tunnel. The front yard was filled with a warm yellow glow from the yard light sitting high on a wooden pole. Kevin could see that most of the lights were on inside the cabin too.

The cabin was made of big old logs painted fire-engine red—Grandma's favorite color. The color got brighter and brighter as they pulled up. The filling between the logs and the trim around the windows was bright white. All eight of the grandkids had helped paint the cabin the previous year. Despite how much work it was, they were happy to help Grandma and Bapoe with this wonderful place.

Dad parked next to the little wooden porch that sat on the front of the cabin. Bapoe opened the cabin door and walked outside to greet them as they piled out of the car.

The first thing Kevin noticed was that it was a little chillier than he had expected for late June. The next thing he noticed was how stiff he was from the long drive. After a quick stretch, raising his hands to the sky, he opened the back of the SUV and grabbed his duffel bag.

Linda rushed to be the first to give Bapoe a big hug, then she headed inside to hug Grandma. Next in line, Kevin dropped his bag and gave Bapoe a big hug himself.

"Welcome to the north country!" Bapoe said with a voice that matched his smile.

Kevin loved Bapoe. He didn't have much hair left—and what he did have was almost all gray. He wore thick glasses and an old gray wool sweater that had a familiar smell of aftershave. He loved hunting and fishing as much as Kevin and Dad did.

Kevin pulled open the cabin door and dragged his big duffel bag inside. By the familiar warmth and the smell of smoke, Kevin knew Bapoe had a crackling fire burning in the fireplace.

Leaving Linda's embrace, Grandma came across the kitchen with a big smile and her arms open wide, ready to hug Kevin.

"Hey, kiddo, how are you?" she asked.

Grandma was one of the most amazing people Kevin knew. Her wavy salt-and-pepper hair was always done up perfectly. She loved wearing red dresses, and her smile could fill any room. Over the years, her warm hugs had soothed away many tears when Kevin had managed to hurt himself doing crazy things. All the grandchildren loved spending time with her. Grandma's positive energy flowed from her as if she were an angel.

After a wonderful hug with Kevin, Grandma went to the door to greet Mom and Dad.

Once the hugs and welcomes were complete, they unpacked the car and settled into the cabin, which was alive with so many great memories. After a bowl of popcorn and some catching up with Grandma and Bapoe, the kids called it a night.

Chapter 2

On Saturday morning, Kevin woke up early, as he always did at the cabin. He walked to the living room, where Bapoe was sitting in his favorite rocking chair. A steaming cup of coffee and two cookies were sitting next to him on a little round table. Together, Kevin and Bapoe enjoyed watching the birds flitting around at the feeder. As they sat, the rising sun began to sparkle across the lake that sat so peacefully at the bottom of the hill.

It wasn't long before the rest of the family was up. Grandma and Mom were busy in the kitchen. From the smell of it, Mom's famous caramel rolls were in the oven. Kevin couldn't wait—he loved eating them right out of the oven, with butter melted all over.

When Mom said the rolls were done, Linda and Kevin raced to the kitchen. As they jostled together, Kevin hip-checked Linda, causing her to nearly lose her balance. With a snicker, Kevin took the opportunity to grab the first plate.

Grandma looked at Kevin. "That wasn't a very nice thing to do to your sister. How do you think that made your friend Jesus feel?"

This caught Kevin a little off guard, but he came up with a zinger. "Jesus will have to get over it—I gotta have the first caramel roll!" he said with a big smirk, thinking he was funny.

Grandma didn't say another word. She just clamped her lips together and let out a soft sigh.

That afternoon, Kevin and Linda were playing slapjack when Bapoe called out, "Who wants to go fishing on the pontoon?"

"I do!" Kevin replied, jumping to his feet. He *loved* fishing!

"Me too!" Linda said.

"You? Really?" Kevin shot at her. "You stink at fishing. You'll just use up all our bait."

"Shut up! That's not true!" Linda shot back.

"Hold on now," Bapoe said, stepping in. He raised his eyebrow at Kevin. "That was no way to talk to your sister. I would be thrilled to have her join us."

"Whatever," Kevin grumbled. He scooted through the kitchen, heading for the door outside.

Grandma was standing at the sink. She stuck her arm out like a crossing guard, stopping Kevin in his tracks. Judging by the look of disappointment on her face, Kevin knew she had overheard everything.

"How do you think your friend Jesus would feel about you talking to your sister like that?" she asked calmly, staring into Kevin's eyes with great concern.

Once again, this caught Kevin off guard. He didn't have a joke this time. "I don't know," he said with a shrug. "It's just that she isn't very good at fishing."

Softening her eyes and shaking her head slowly, Grandma lowered her arm without saying another word.

Kevin turned and continued toward the door, but Grandma's disappointment lingered in his mind and made him feel uneasy. He didn't like disappointing her.

And he wasn't sure what was up with the "your friend Jesus" stuff. Kevin went to church with his family most Sundays and attended religion classes—though he never really paid attention. So this talk about Jesus seemed a little strange.

After dinner, Grandma read in the living room, as usual. She had a candle burning on the table next to her. Kevin was amazed at how peaceful she looked.

"What are you reading?" he asked, curious.

She gave him a calm smile. "I'm reading about my friend Jesus."

There it was again! Not wanting anything to do with that, Kevin simply said, "Oh," and went over to sit by Bapoe instead.

When Sunday morning came, Grandma and Bapoe got ready for church.

"Your mom and dad have some packing to do, but do you two want to join us for church?" Grandma asked Linda and Kevin.

"Sure!" Linda chimed in.

Kevin, however, wasn't excited about the idea. He didn't want to miss out on cabin fun.

"No," he said slowly. "I think I'll stay here."

On their way out the door, Grandma softly pulled Kevin to the side. "I'll say hi to our friend Jesus and His Father for you when I'm at church," she whispered.

"Okay . . ." Kevin said, a little confused.

Later that evening, everyone said goodbye to Mom and Dad, who were heading back home for the week. Kevin and Linda were excited for their time alone with Grandma and Bapoe.

As Dad's SUV disappeared down the driveway, Grandma, Bapoe, and the kids gathered around the kitchen table to play Skip-Bo, one of their favorite card games. After a few hands, Kevin went to the fridge to grab a Sprite.

"Hey, could you get me one too, please?" Linda asked from the table.

Kevin closed the fridge door, waltzed back to the table, cracked open his soda, and looked right at her. "Get it yourself," he said. "I'm not your servant."

Instantly, Grandma put her hand on Kevin's arm. "How do you think that makes your friend Jesus feel?"

Kevin should have seen the Jesus thing coming, but it still took him by surprise. He tried to recover. "Well, Jesus isn't here, so He won't mind if Linda has to get her own soda."

"Kevin," Grandma said firmly, "Jesus is everywhere and in everyone's heart, whether they realize it or not. Now *get up*, go back to that fridge, and get your sister a soda."

By Grandma's piercing stare and stern tone of voice, Kevin knew she meant business. He quickly hurried back to the fridge. When he returned, he carefully handed a soda to Linda.

"Why, thank you, Kevin. That was very nice of you," Linda said with a fake smile.

Kevin picked up his cards and tried to avoid making eye contact with anyone, but Grandma wasn't finished.

"Now Kevin," she continued, "if you had chosen to get her that soda on your own, you could have enjoyed the feeling of love in your heart, knowing you'd done something nice for someone. But there is no love when you do something only because someone else told you to," she added with a disappointed frown.

After the card game, Grandma made her way to her chair in the living room and lit her candle. She peacefully began reading once again.

Kevin was on his laptop in the kitchen, playing a game. He couldn't help but look up and watch Grandma for a second.

Bapoe happened to walk by and see Kevin watching her. "She sure does love reading about our friend Jesus in that Bible," Bapoe told him quietly.

Kevin quickly looked down at his game. But in the back of his mind, he had to admit that this Jesus thing was making him wonder.

Chapter 3

When Kevin sat up in bed the next morning, the sun was sparkling through the window. He could hear people talking and plates clanging in the kitchen. He must have slept in longer than usual. He crawled out of bed and got dressed.

Making his way to the kitchen, he was overtaken by the smell of bacon. His favorite! He found Grandma and Linda smiling, talking, and cooking away.

"Good morning, kiddo!" Grandma said. She walked over and gave him a big warm hug.

"Morning, Kev," Linda said, grinning. "We are making you and Bapoe breakfast. We made your favorite—bacon and pancakes with chocolate chips. They are just about ready. We also have Bapoe's eggs over easy, plus crispy hash browns, just as he likes them."

Kevin was a little confused. "What's the special occasion?"

Grandma gave Linda a squeeze across the shoulders. "It was all your sister's idea. She simply wanted to do something nice for you boys."

"Yep," Linda said. "What better way to start the day than by pleasing my friend

Jesus and doing something kind?" Her face broke into a sly but proud smile, as if she were revealing a big secret.

"*What?*" Kevin sputtered. Now even Linda was saying it?

Linda laughed. "Grandma introduced me to Jesus a couple of years ago. Once you really understand who He is, it's pretty cool." She winked at Grandma.

Kevin just shook his head and sat down at the kitchen table. He picked up a piece of bacon and took a bite. The salty-sweet taste was fantastic.

"All I can say is, thank you, Jesus—this bacon is amazing!" He chewed with a big smile on his face.

Grandma and Linda shared a knowing look.

Later that day, Kevin headed outside. Kevin's whole family loved hunting, so one of his favorite things to do at the cabin was to practice with his BB gun. The old wooden fence along the edge of the yard was the perfect spot away from the cabin. Kevin placed some soda cans on the top rail. He was a great shot and loved making the cans jump.

While he was shooting, a couple of tiny chickadees landed on the oak tree next to the fence. Seeing the challenge, Kevin quickly aimed at one of them. With a perfect shot, he hit the tiny bird. It dropped to the ground.

Surprised and excited, Kevin ran over to pick up the lifeless bird. He was proud of the shot. Not many people could have made that one.

As he was examining the black and white feathers, Kevin heard the cabin door open. In a panic, he quickly tossed the bird into the woods and walked back to the cabin, trying to be nonchalant.

Grandma was sitting on the front steps with a cup of coffee. Feeling a little guilty now, Kevin hoped she hadn't been looking out the window when he made the shot.

He walked over and sat down next to her. "Hey, Grandma, what's up?" he asked, trying to keep his voice steady.

She smiled and shrugged. "Oh, I knew you were shooting your BB gun, so I thought I'd come out to watch. I know you're very good at hitting those cans."

Kevin relaxed a little. She didn't seem to know.

"Yeah, I can make them fly," he said. He stood up, pumped his BB gun, took aim at a can, and plunked it.

"Great shot, kiddo!"

"Thanks."

"By the way," she said, drawing out her words slowly, "do you know what Bapoe's favorite thing to do in the early morning is?"

Kevin's face instantly filled with red heat. He knew exactly where she was going with this.

"It's sitting in the living room, drinking his coffee, while looking at the birds on the feeder." She gazed out in the direction of the oak tree, where Kevin had shot the chickadee. "He sure does love those birds. I believe one of the reasons God put birds here was for Bapoe to enjoy."

Kevin swallowed hard and looked down at the grass. He knew he was busted.

As Grandma rose up and headed back inside, she turned and added one more thing: "You know, even when no one else is looking, your friend Jesus is always with you."

Kevin just stood there and watched the door close behind Grandma. He felt awful now about shooting the bird. How mad would Bapoe be if he found out? And could Jesus *really* be watching all the time?

Later that night, Grandma was back in her chair, reading her Bible with the candle burning. Linda was curled up on the couch, reading a book, and Kevin was getting ready to dive into his computer game. But then his curiosity got the best of him. He went over to Grandma.

"So . . ." he said, "what's all this Jesus stuff about?"

A smile grew on Linda's face, though she didn't look up from her book.

Grandma carefully set her Bible down. Without the slightest change to her peaceful face, she looked at Kevin.

"Well, what would you like to know?" she asked.

"I don't know," Kevin said. He didn't have the foggiest idea.

"Well, how about we start with this: Do you believe Jesus is real?" Grandma carefully asked with a tilted head and focused but soft eyes.

Kevin shrugged a little. "I guess so. I mean, I hear about Him all the time at my religion classes and at church. But I've never really given it much thought," he admitted.

This gave Grandma a wonderful opportunity to carefully explain all the facts behind Jesus. She said that Jesus lived over two thousand years ago. He was human, just like us. But He was also the Son of God and one with the Father. God sent Him to be born on earth as a human so that He could be the salvation of the world.

She explained that followers of Jesus—like Luke, Paul, and many others—wrote wonderful stories about Him. Those stories were brought together and put into a book called the New Testament of the Bible. And hundreds of years before Jesus was born, stories had been written about how He would be born. These stories are in the section of the Bible called the Old Testament.

So, when Jesus's birth matched those older stories, it was more proof for us to believe.

Kevin was amazed. He looked over at Grandma's Bible sitting on the little table. His eyes locked onto it as if he were seeing it for the first time.

Grandma then told Kevin about the many miracles Jesus performed to show people He was one with God. He turned water into wine. He fed thousands of people with only two fish and five loaves of bread. He gave sight to the blind and healed the sick. And even more amazingly, He brought several people back from the dead. With each of the miracles, many people began to believe that Jesus was truly the Son of God.

Kevin had never heard anyone describe Jesus the way Grandma did. Her words were so real. It was like she was telling him about her grandfather or great-grandfather. She made Jesus sound like someone she knew very well and loved very much.

She also explained that Jesus told His twelve friends, the disciples, that God had a plan for Him. He would die, but then, on the third day, He would rise again. This would be the final miracle that would show all humankind that Jesus was one with God.

And so, Jesus suffered a terrible death on the cross and then was laid to rest in a tomb. On the third day, just as He had said, He was raised from the dead. Over five hundred people saw Him after He was resurrected.

"Jesus did this for us—for you, for me, for everyone," Grandma said. "He died for our sins so that we could be with Him and His Father in heaven. And while we're here on earth, He's always with us, always in our hearts, always guiding us to be like Him, and always forgiving us when we fall short. That's why He's our friend."

Kevin just sat there, his mouth half-open, letting his grandma's words sink in.

"Well, what do you think, kiddo?" Grandma asked, looking deeply into Kevin's eyes.

"Wow." For a long time, that was all he could say. "No one ever explained it to me like that, Grandma," he finally added.

"Or maybe they did, but you weren't ready to listen," Grandma said in her simple way. She reached over and hugged him. "But I have a feeling you're ready now to learn about your friend Jesus."

Kevin nodded. Something was happening inside him. He just didn't know what yet.

Chapter 4

Kevin woke early the next morning. He strolled out to the living room, where Bapoe was quietly gazing out the window.

"Good morning, Bapoe. Watching the birds again?" Kevin asked.

"Yes, I am—and I'm spending some quiet time with my friend Jesus." Bapoe gave Kevin a warm smile and a wink. "I find that the combination of a quiet morning, sunshine, and birds creates the perfect setting to have a nice chat with Jesus. We tend to get along good in the mornings."

Kevin just sat and looked out the window, letting the words sink in. Even Bapoe had a friendship with Jesus.

Soon, bacon was on Kevin's mind. Grandma was in the kitchen and clearly at it again, as the cabin started to fill with wonderful breakfast smells.

"Good morning," Kevin greeted her.

"Good morning, kiddo." She smiled. "Grab a plate."

He did, and she quickly loaded it up with pancakes, bacon, and watermelon. It was a good morning for Kevin.

Bapoe joined Kevin at the table. They were already enjoying their breakfast when Linda came strolling in. She still looked tired, with tangled hair and half-opened eyes.

"Morning," she said with a groggy voice.

"Good morning, princess," Bapoe said, lighting up.

"I hope you're ready for a wonderful breakfast," Grandma said.

"Geez, you should see your hair!" Kevin smart-mouthed.

Instantly, the positive energy Grandma and Bapoe had created was crushed.

Before Linda could even react, Grandma gave Kevin a look of great curiosity. "Kevin, how do you think that comment made your friend Jesus feel?"

Kevin felt as if he had been caught with his hand in the cookie jar. Grandma was right. That wasn't how Jesus wanted him to treat his sister. He understood that now.

So, Kevin decided to turn the situation around.

"What I meant was—boy, you must have slept *really* well!" he said with a big grin.

Linda just shook her head and grabbed a plate. Grandma and Bapoe glanced at each other and smiled.

That was the start to the new Kevin. All throughout the day, Grandma's voice was inside his head. Whatever Kevin did or said, that voice kept reminding him, "How would that make your friend Jesus feel?"

The crazy thing was, it turned out to be one of the best days ever. He and Linda got along great because he wasn't constantly picking on her. He was actually happy when Linda decided to go out fishing with him and Bapoe. And when he was out shooting the BB gun, he felt so good to just watch the chickadees fly around. All these little things were building positive momentum.

After dinner, Kevin was eager to sit with Grandma and learn more about Jesus. She pulled Kevin close to her on the couch.

"Would you like to hear some of my favorite Bible verses?" Grandma asked.

Kevin nodded with a happy smile.

Grandma opened her Bible. Kevin was amazed at how many pencil marks and yellow sticky notes were scattered throughout the pages. She even had little notes written in the margins. It looked like something he would see his teachers using in school to teach the day's lesson.

"OK," Grandma said. "I'm going to start with one of the most important verses, which is John 3:16: 'God loved the world so much that he gave his one and only Son, so that everyone who believes in him would not perish but have eternal life.' Do you know what that means?" she asked with a mix of seriousness and excitement in her eyes.

"Not really," Kevin admitted.

"Remember how we talked last night about Jesus being God's only Son and being sent to earth to save us all? Well, it is said many times in the Bible that if we believe in Jesus and follow His teachings, we will go to heaven and have eternal life." She gave Kevin a little nudge in the side. "I don't know about you, kiddo, but I want to go to heaven. And I would really like to see you there one day too."

That hit home for Kevin. He knew Grandma would surely be in heaven. And he thought it would be really cool if he could spend eternity with her there. Just thinking of it made his eyes light up.

"How about this one from John 15:12?" Grandma continued. "'My command is this: love each other as I have loved you.' Jesus said this to his disciples. It's a very important lesson he wanted to leave them before he was to be killed."

"Grandma, are these Jesus's actual words?" Kevin asked. "The way it's written, it sounds as if it's straight from Him."

"Great question, kiddo. All the writings are inspired by Jesus. They are meant to teach us lessons that Jesus wanted us to learn. In John 14, verses 6 and 7, Jesus said, 'I am the way and the truth and the life. No one comes to the Father except through me. If you really know me, you will know my Father as well.' And then let's follow that with John 14:21: 'Whoever has my commands and keeps them is the one who loves me. The one who loves me will be loved by my Father, and I too will love them and show myself to them.'"

Grandma stopped to glance at Kevin. He was nodding slowly, taking it all in.

"These are some very important words," she said. "They tell us that we must know, believe, and love Jesus in order to be close to God. It also tells us that if we really love Jesus, we will obey His lessons. I find reading the Bible is the best way for me to get to know Jesus. And the more I get to know Him, the more love I have in my heart. And that helps me treat people better."

Grandma and Kevin spent the whole evening going through Bible verses. Grandma did a wonderful job talking through the verses and answering Kevin's questions. He was beginning to understand just how important Jesus was to his life.

For the rest of the week, Grandma and Kevin spent every evening reading the Bible and talking about what they had read. Linda joined them. She wanted to learn more about Jesus—and she wanted some Grandma time too.

It was one of the most important weeks of Kevin's life. Learning about Jesus, His lessons, and how He was the key to getting to heaven—it was life changing.

Chapter 5

When Mom and Dad arrived at the cabin Friday night, Kevin and Linda jumped from the couch and ran to the door to greet them. The kids were eager to fill Mom and Dad in on all the fun they'd had at the cabin that week.

Mom and Dad loved hearing about the kids catching fish and making forts and how perfect the water had been for swimming all week. But they couldn't hide their surprise when they heard that the kids—Kevin included—had spent their evenings reading the Bible and learning about Jesus.

"Grandma taught us about the many miracles Jesus performed," Linda said excitedly. "And then the most amazing miracle of all happened: Kevin was nice to me!"

Everyone, especially Kevin, laughed at that one.

Mom gave Kevin a big hug. "I never doubted you for a second. Well, maybe a *second*."

Kevin laughed again. For the first time, he understood why Linda, his parents, and his teachers were sometimes frustrated with him. He was a pretty good kid, but he didn't always make the right choices in how he treated people. But now that he knew about his friend Jesus, things would be different.

The next day, Mom and Dad were once again surprised. They couldn't believe the change in Kevin. They noticed his happy greetings in the morning, his offer to help with the dishes, his pleases and thank-yous, and, of course, his kindness toward his sister. Little choices seemed to be making big differences for Kevin.

Sunday morning came, which meant the magical time at the cabin was coming to a close. Kevin couldn't believe how fast time had flown.

The familiar smell of coffee filled the cabin. As usual, Grandma and Bapoe emerged out of their room dressed for church.

"Good morning, kiddo," she said to Kevin. "How are you doing on this glorious morning?"

"I'm doing great. Though I'm just a little sad that we have to go home today," he added.

"Oh, me too. Bapoe and I will sure miss you and your sister. Speaking of you and your sister, would you guys like to join us at church? It's a great way to visit and honor our friend Jesus as well as His Father. The church is considered God's house. So, going to church is like visiting our friend at His own house. It's our special chance to spend time with Him."

Kevin shook his head in amazement. "I don't know how you do it, Grandma. Now you're even making church sound cool. I'm in!"

"Me too!" Linda said. "Mom, Dad—are you guys coming to church with us?" she asked with contagious excitement.

Dad gave Mom a confused but happy look. "Whose kids *are* these?"

She threw her hands up. "I'm not sure what's going on, but I like it! Let's all go to church!"

Bapoe walked over and gave Grandma a peck on her cheek. "You are one special lady," he whispered to her. "And I can only imagine how you make our friend Jesus feel."

Chapter 6

Before Kevin knew it, it was Labor Day weekend, which marked the final days of summer vacation and the final visit to the cabin. The whole family was excited to spend three days with Grandma and Bapoe.

Bapoe, Dad, and the kids spent hours on the pontoon, pulling in bass and sunfish. The fish were biting like crazy. The lake water was warm and clear, perfect for swimming too.

In the evenings, after their wonderful family dinners, Kevin and Linda shared their

Grandma time. She would read a passage from the Bible, and the three of them would talk about it.

Kevin was still so mesmerized by how Grandma explained the stories. From her years of reading the Bible, she even knew how different stories fit together.

By Labor Day afternoon, the family was all packed up and ready to head home. That final day had come sooner than Kevin would have liked.

While Linda was enjoying some last moments with Bapoe, Kevin sat down with Grandma for one more Bible story. She told him how Jesus tried to get people to understand the right way to live. But not everyone listened—even after He performed so many miracles. Some people refused to believe in

Him. Kevin found that very frustrating and confusing.

"I don't get it," he said. "How could they *not* believe in Him?"

"You have to remember that God had a plan," Grandma explained. "Yes, the people who didn't believe in Jesus sent Him to a horrible death, but that allowed Jesus to sacrifice Himself for us. And no one has performed a greater miracle than God raising Jesus from the dead. That one amazing act caused Christianity to spread around the world."

Kevin nodded. The more he learned and read from the Bible, the closer he felt to Jesus.

Grandma set the Bible down. She looked at Kevin and put one hand on his shoulder.

"This summer, you learned a lot about Jesus and what He expects of us. Tomorrow is a big day—the first day of school. You'll be in eighth grade. I encourage you to pray each day, asking Jesus to help and guide you. You'll have many choices to make in your life. If you allow Jesus to help you along the way, I'm confident He'll help you make good choices. Most importantly, remember to *treat others as you want to be treated*. Nothing will make your friend Jesus happier." She gave him a warm smile, and a tear came to her eye. "I love you very much, Kevin!"

"I love you too, Grandma."

Kevin felt a joy he had never felt before. He knew it was the love of Jesus filling his heart.

Last hugs were given, and last good-byes were said. Dad settled into the driver's seat, Mom sat in front with her book, and Kevin and Linda slid into the back seat. They shared a sad little smile to be heading home after a wonderful time.

As the cabin faded behind them, Kevin snuggled into his pillow against the door. Closing his eyes, he thought about everything he'd learned from Grandma. A smile grew on his face.

He felt different. Excitement brewed inside him. His heart was filled with positive energy, and he pictured bringing it to school with him. He *would* treat others as he wanted to be treated. He pictured how amazing school would be if everyone did that.

His mind was set. He was bound and determined to make Jesus proud. And he knew that would make his grandma proud too.

This will be the best year ever! he thought as he peeked out the window at the sky above. *Just you watch, Jesus!*

† † †

One bright light inside someone's heart can spread like the rising sun. Like Kevin, *you* could choose to be that light. How do you think your light could impact your family, your friends, your school? More importantly, how do you think it would make your friend Jesus feel?

More from Grandma

Morning Prayer

God, thank you for this wonderful day. I am grateful for everything you have done for me and given me. Thank you, Jesus, for being with me always. Help me make great choices today and treat everyone as I want to be treated. Help me shine brightly and make you proud. Amen.

More Great Bible Verses

"Let your light shine before others, that they may see your good deeds and glorify your Father in heaven." (Matthew 5:16)

"Jesus replied: 'Love the Lord your God with all your heart and with all your soul and with all your mind.' This is the first and greatest commandment. And the second is like it: 'Love your neighbor as yourself.'" (Matthew 22:37–40)

"Jesus answered him, 'I am the way and the truth and the life. No one comes to the Father except through me.'" (John 14:6)

"Ask and it will be given to you; seek and you will find; knock and the door will be opened to you. For everyone who asks receives; the one who seeks finds; and to the one who knocks, the door will be opened." (Matthew 7:7–8)

"You have heard that it was said, 'Love your neighbor and hate your enemy.' But I tell you, love your enemies and pray for those who persecute you." (Matthew 5:43–44)

"For I am the Lord your God who takes hold of your right hand and says to you, Do not fear; I will help you." (Isaiah 41:13)

"Each of you should use whatever gift you have received to serve others, as faithful stewards of God's grace in its various forms." (1 Peter 4:10)

"Do not let any unwholesome talk come out of your mouths, but only what is helpful for building others up . . ." (Ephesians 4:29)

"Do not judge, or you too will be judged." (Matthew 7:1)

"A new command I give you: Love one another. As I have loved you, so you must love one another." (John 13:34)

About the Author

Minnesota native and outdoor enthusiast, Kevin Lovegreen loves inspiring kids. He is well known for his award-winning book series, *Lucky Luke's Hunting Adventures*, and his engaging school presentations around the country. Kevin is on an exciting, faith-based adventure and wants you to come along for the journey with his new book, *Grandma Introduced Me To My Friend Jesus*, delivered to him by God. You can see all his books and learn more about his presentations by visiting his website.